ADA TWIST, SCIENTIST

by **Andrea Beaty**

illustrated by **David Roberts**

Abrams Books for Young Readers, New York

ADA MARIE! ADA MARIE!

Said not a word till the day she turned three.

She bounced in her crib and looked all around,

observing the world but not making a sound.

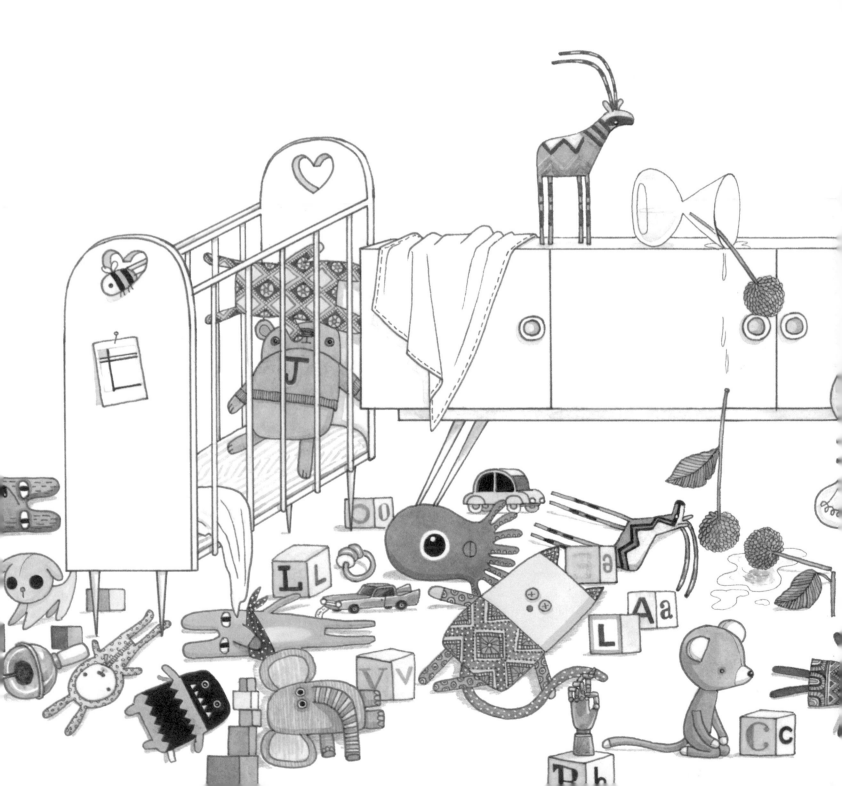

She learned how to climb and made her big break,

with a trail of chaos left in her wake.

She ran through the day chasing each sound and sight,

and didn't slow down till she conked out at night.

Her parents were frazzled—but tried not to freak—

as Ada grew bigger and *still* did not speak.

Clearly, young Ada, with lots in her head,

would have something to say when it ought to be said.

That's just what happened when Ada turned three.

She tore through the house on a fact-finding spree

and climbed up the clock, just as high as she could.

Her parents yelled,

"STOP!"

(as all good parents would).

Ada's chin quivered,
but she did not cry.
She took a deep breath
and she simply asked,
"Why?"

"Why does it tick and why does it tock?"

"Why don't we call it a grand*daughter* clock?"

"Why are there pointy things stuck to a rose?"

"Why are there hairs up inside of your nose?"

She started with *Why?* and then *What? How?* and *When?*

By bedtime she came back to *Why?* once again.

She drifted to sleep as her dazed parents smiled

at the curious thoughts of their curious child,

who wanted to know what the world was about.

They kissed her and whispered, "You'll figure it out."

Her parents kept up with their high-flying kid,

whose questions and chaos both grew as she did.

Even Miss Greer found her hands were quite full
when young Ada's chaos wreaked havoc at school.
But this much was clear about Miss Ada Twist:
She had all the traits of a great scientist.

Ada was busy that first day of spring,

testing the sounds that make mockingbirds sing,

when a horrible stench whacked her right in the nose—

a pungent aroma that curled up her toes.

"Zowie!" said Ada, which got her to thinking:

"What is the source of that terrible stinking?"

"How does a nose know there's something to smell?"

"And does it still stink if there's no nose to tell?"

She rattled off questions and tapped on her chin.

She'd start at the start, where she ought to begin.

A mystery! A riddle! A puzzle! A quest!

This was the moment that Ada loved best.

Ada did research to learn all she could

of smelling and smells—both the stinky and good.

One hypothesis Ada thought could be true:

The terrible stink came from Dad's cabbage stew!

She tested and tested, but soon Ada knew . . .

it was time to come up with Hypothesis Two.

Then *ZOWIE!* The stink struck again, just like that!

Hypothesis Two: "It's caused by the cat."

The cat couldn't make such a stink on its own.

It needed perfume and some fancy cologne.

So Young Ada tested. The test was a flop.

She started again, but her parents yelled,

"STOP!"

"ADA MARIE! ADA MARIE!

To the Thinking Chair—NOW! By the time we count THREE!"

"Enough!" said her mother. "That's it!" said her dad.

Her parents were frustrated, frazzled, and mad.

"Why—?" Ada questioned.

Her mother said, "NO!"

"What—?" Ada queried.

Her father said, "GO!"

"You've ruined our supper! You've made the cat stink!

Enough with your questions! Now sit there and THINK!"

She looked at her parents. Her heart turned to goo.

Poor Ada Twist didn't know what to do.

She sat all alone, by herself in the hall.

And Ada, once more, could say nothing at all.

And so Ada sat

and she sat

and she sat

and she thought about science and stew and the cat

and how her experiments made such a big mess.

"Does it have to be so? Is that part of success?

Are messes a problem?" And while she was thinking . . .

What *WAS* the source of that terrible stinking?

Ada Marie did what scientists do:

She asked a small question, and then she asked two.

And each of those led her to three questions more,

and some of *those* questions resulted in four.

As Ada got thinking, she really dug in.

She scribbled her questions and tapped on her chin.

She started at *Why?* and then *What? How?* and *When?*

At the end of the hall she reached *Why?* once again.

Her parents calmed down, and they came back to talk.

They looked at the hallway and just had to gawk.

No patch of bare paint could be seen on the wall.

The Thinking Chair now was the Great Thinking Hall.

They watched their young daughter and sighed as they did.

What would they do with this curious kid,

who wanted to know what the world was about?

They smiled and whispered, "We'll figure it out."

And that's what they did—because that's what you do

when your kid has a passion and heart that is true.

They remade their world—now they're all in the act

of helping young Ada sort fiction from fact.

She asks lots of questions. How could she resist?

It's all in the heart of a young scientist.

And as for that smell? What can Ada Twist do

but learn all she can with her friends in grade two?

Will they discover the stink that curls toes?

Well, that is the question.

And someday . . .

Who knows?

Edward's book
—A.B.

For my nephew Joel
—D.R.

A NOTE FROM THE AUTHOR

Women have been scientists for as long as there has been science. They've asked questions and looked for answers to the secrets of the universe. Of soil and stars. Stalactites and seahorses. Glaciers and gravity. Brains and black holes. Of everything.

Ada Marie Twist is named for two of the many women whose curiosity and passion led them to make great discoveries. Marie Curie discovered the elements polonium and radium, and her work led to the invention of X-rays. Ada Lovelace was a mathematician and the very first computer programmer.

The illustrations in this book were made with watercolors, pen, and ink on Arches paper. For some pieces, pencil and graph paper were also employed.

Cataloging-in-Publication Data has been applied for and may be obtained from the Library of Congress.
ISBN: 978-1-4197-2137-3

Printed and bound in U.S.A.
10 9 8 7 6 5 4 3 2 1

Abrams Books for Young Readers are available at special discounts when purchased in quantity for premiums and promotions as well as fundraising or educational use. Special editions can also be created to specification. For details, contact specialsales@abramsbooks.com or the address below.

ABRAMS The Art of Books
115 West 18th Street, New York, NY 10011
abramsbooks.com